Big Sister BAABARA

For Sage – here we go again! – C.G.

HODDER CHILDREN'S BOOKS

First published in Great Britain in 2020 by Hodder and Stoughton

Text and illustrations © Caroline Gray, 2020

The moral rights of the author-illustrator have been asserted.

All rights reserved.

A CIP catalogue record for this book is available from the British Library.

HB ISBN 978 1 444 92948 5
PB ISBN 978 1 444 92949 2

1 3 5 7 9 10 8 6 4 2

Printed and bound in China.

MIX
Paper from responsible sources
FSC
www.fsc.org   FSC® C104740

Hodder Children's Books
An imprint of
Hachette Children's Group
Part of Hodder and Stoughton

Carmelite House, 50 Victoria Embankment, London, EC4Y 0DZ

An Hachette UK Company

www.hachette.co.uk
www.hachettechildrens.co.uk

Big Sister BAABARA

Caroline Gray

Hodder
Children's
Books

In the quiet village of Chew-upon-Cud, there lived
a sweet little lamb by the name of Baabara Muttons.

Baabara had everything a young sheep could wish for:
grown-ups to take care of her, lots of nice things
to eat and a cuddly cow called Loula Belle.

There was just ONE thing missing from Baabara's life. More than anything in the world, she wanted to be . . .

A BIG SISTER

(to an actual, real-life baby).

I would **LOVE** it

and **SQUEEZE** it

and we'd be the bestest friends in
the Whole Wide World, thought Baabara.

Well, sometimes wishes really do come true.

A baby was on the way!

As the months went by, Baabara's excitement grew . . .

. . . and **grew!**

Until, at last, the big day came . . .

"They're here!"

There in the crib was a big, BIG surprise:

not ONE,

not TWO,

not THREE,

not even FOUR . . .

but FIVE

new brothers and sisters.

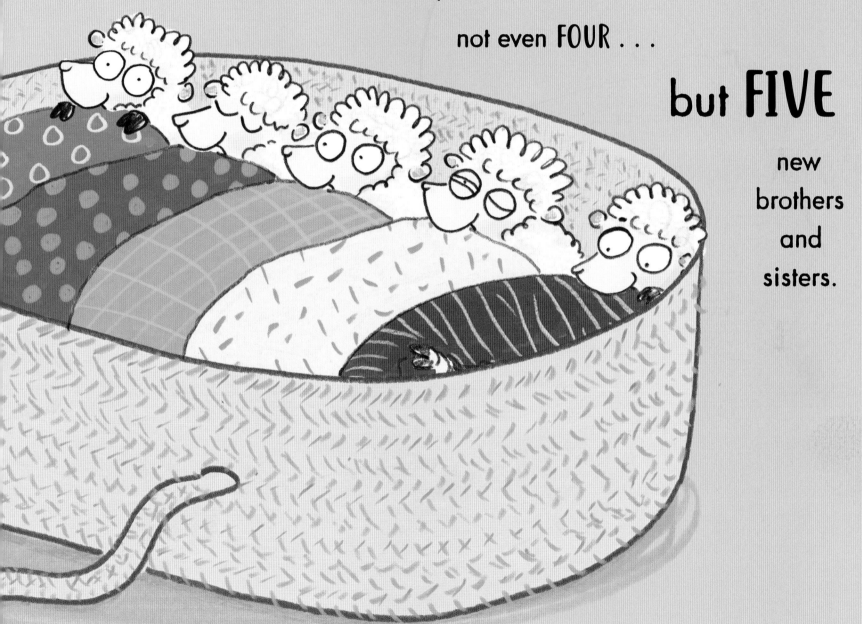

"We're going to be BEST FRIENDS," Baabara whispered.

Baabara made every effort to impress the new arrivals.

But they were a difficult crowd to please.

"Have patience," her parents told her. "They're still too small to play, but before you know it, they will be big just like you."

How long is THAT going to take? thought Baabara.

Being a big sister wasn't nearly as much fun as she'd expected.

But the babies DID grow – and that was worse!

First there was the MESS. They CHEWED
and SPLATTED and DRIBBLED all day long.

Then there was the NOISE. They BLEATED and BAAED
and CRASHED and BANGED from noon till night.

Enough is enough, thought Baabara.

These babies have got to GO!

But . . . where?!

Nana and Pop-Pop
wouldn't take them.

The charity bins were
full to bursting.

And the neighbours
had more than enough
kids of their own.

But then, a very, very clever idea
popped into Baabara's head.

"Just nipping to the post office, Mama,"
said Baabara. "I won't be long."

Mrs Piggles was surprised
to see Baabara.
"Are you here to post a
letter, dear?" she asked.

"I would like to send THIS to New Zealand,"
said Baabara, and she handed
over a BIG, HEAVY box.

Peace at last, she thought.
No more babies!

Back at home, everything was lovely and quiet.

"Just me, myself and I,"
sang Baabara.

There was no one to mess up her room. Or ruin
her toys. Or spoil her games. It was PERFECT.

So why was her wool standing on end
and fear nibbling at her hooves?

What if . . .?

Baabara knew she had made a big, BIG mistake!

"Mama, quick! We have to go to the post office!"

Baabara tumbled through the
door of the post office and . . .

There they were!

Mrs Piggles had NOT posted the package.

"I thought you might be back, Baabara," she said.

TO: NEW ZEALAND
FROM: BAABARA'S HOUSE

Baabara squeezed her brothers and sisters SO tightly and they all squeezed her right back.

"I love you," she whispered.

"And I'll always take care of you."

And from that day on, Baabara was the best
big sister in the Whole Wide World.

Well . . .